This is my Book

Her

THIS BOOK BELONGS TO

Cassandra Cassandra

Her

Chris Chris

GIVEN BY

Morgan

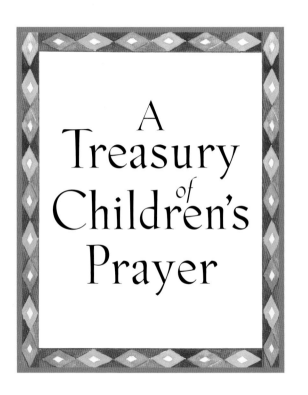

A Treasury *of* Children's Prayer

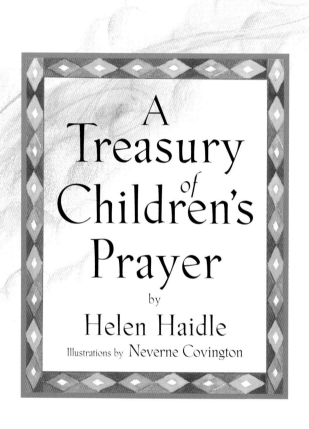

A Treasury *of* Children's Prayer

by

Helen Haidle

Illustrations by Neverne Covington

Zonder**kidz**

A Treasury of Children's Prayer
ISBN: 0-310-70030-2
Copyright © 2002 by Helen Haidle

Zonder**kidz**™

The children's group of Zondervan

Requests for information should be addressed to:
Grand Rapids, Michigan 49530
www.zonderkidz.com

All Scripture quotations, unless otherwise indicated, are taken from Holy Bible,
New International Reader's Version ® Copyright © 1994, 1996 by International Bible
Society. Used by permission of Zondervan. All rights reserved.

Edited by: Gwen Ellis
Art by: Neverne Covington
Art direction by: Lisa Workman & Laura Maitner

Printed in China

03 04 05/HK/5 4 3

Dedication

To all the great 4th - 6th graders
Of my Sunday school class in Sisters, Oregon.
Kamm Akaka, Rebecca Akaka, Angela Barry,
Randy Huff, Nathan Jackson, Erin Kanzig,
Jordan Kolb, Ashley Lanphear, Rebeccah Lovegren,
Emery Meyer, Eric Mickel, Kyle Rickards,
Jena Rickards, and Rachael Tenneson.

You are all part of this book—you prayed while I wrote it.
Keep up all your prayers for other people.
You make a big difference in this world!

With extra thanks to Eric Mickel
For the wisdom and insights he shared.

Contents

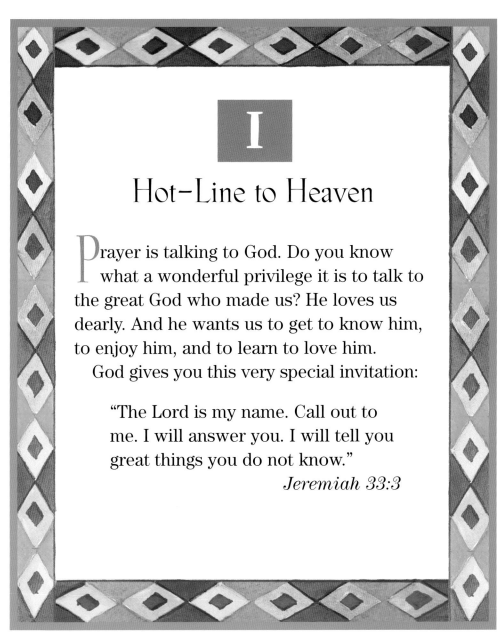

I

Hot-Line to Heaven

Prayer is talking to God. Do you know what a wonderful privilege it is to talk to the great God who made us? He loves us dearly. And he wants us to get to know him, to enjoy him, and to learn to love him.

God gives you this very special invitation:

> "The Lord is my name. Call out to me. I will answer you. I will tell you great things you do not know."
>
> *Jeremiah 33:3*

God invites us to pray! This is the first and best reason for prayer. He is waiting to hear from you. Will you accept God's invitation? Even though God is invisible and you can't see him, he is right there with you. Talk to him just like you would talk to someone you can see.

Talking on the Phone

Aren't you glad when someone takes time to call and talk to you on the telephone?

- Think about when you talk to your grandparents on the phone?

- Think about when you talk on the phone with a friend?

Even though you can't see your grandparent or a friend, you know someone is there on the other end of the line. The person you are talking to may be on the other side of town or perhaps all the way across the country. But you can talk just fine. It is like that when you are praying to God. Even though you can't see God, you can talk to him just fine.

God knows, hears, and sees everything. It is no trouble for God to listen to all of us at the same time. You don't have to wait for God to finish listening to someone else before he listens to you.

Sometimes prayer is like talking on a telephone. But other times prayer is much different than an ordinary phone call.

Sometimes when you call someone, problems happen to keep you from talking. But when you pray to God, you can be sure:

- God is never asleep or away on vacation.
- You won't get a busy signal.
- Your call won't be disconnected.
- God won't ignore you or hang up on you.
- There is no charge. Every prayer is free.
- When God says something is going to happen, it will!

God can do anything!

Prayer Starter

Dear God, I'm glad you love me so much and invite me to pray to you. I'd like to tell you what's happening in my life today.

Hot-Line to Heaven

- Decorate a shoebox or other small box.
- Set out a handful of file cards and pencils.
- Write one prayer request on a single card.
- Write today's date on each card.
- Pray about each request.
- Thank God for hearing you.
- Place all the cards in the prayer box.
- After meals or before bed, pray over the requests again.
- Later on you will be able to write dates when your prayers are answered.

Treasure Nuggets from God's Word

"Come near to God and he will come near to you."

James 4:8

"God has listened . . . He has accepted my prayer."

Psalm 66:19-20

"The Lord is ready to help all those who call out to him."

Psalm 145:18

"Our God . . . we're asking you to [answer our prayers] because you love us so much."

Daniel 9:18

2

Prayer Helps Us Know God

We pray because God wants all of his children to talk to him—every day and at any time. You are God's child because he made you. You are God's child because Jesus died for you.

The more you talk to God, the more you will know him. When you spend time with other people, you become friends with them. And when you spend time in prayer with God, you become friends with him too.

How Important is God to You?

- Do you enjoy God?
- Do you spend time with him?
- Do you talk to God about funny or sad things that happen?
- Do you tell God your thoughts and feelings?
- Do you ask God to help you with your problems?

What Should I Say to God?

God should be the most important person in your life, but maybe you haven't spent much time praying to him. Now would probably be a very good time to start talking to him. God loves you just as you are. He knows what you're thinking, so you can be completely honest when you pray.

- If you have a need, ask God to help.
- When you've done something wrong, ask God to forgive you. Remember, he already knows what you've done.
- You can even tell God when you feel angry or upset.

David told God, "Lord, you know all about me . . . even before I speak a word, you know all about it."

Psalm 139:1, 4

It doesn't matter if you talk out loud, whisper, or pray silently. God knows everything you think or say—even before you say it.

- Tell God "Good Morning" when you wake up.
- Share your thoughts and feelings all during the day.
- Before you fall asleep, talk to God about your day.

What Do You Want?

Matthew 20:29-34

Once two blind men sat beside the road. When they heard that Jesus was near, they shouted, "Lord! Have mercy on us!"

The crowd told them to be quiet. But the two men shouted even louder, "Lord! Have mercy on us!"

When Jesus heard their cries, he stopped and asked them, "What do you want me to do for you?"

The blind men answered, "Lord, we want to be able to see."

Do you think Jesus answered their request? Yes, he did. He loved them, so he touched their eyes. Immediately they could see clearly!

What about you? What would you say if Jesus stood in front of you and asked, "What do you want me to do for you?"

Take-A-Turn Prayer

Gather some friends or your sisters and brothers together. Read David's prayer in Psalm 139. Then take turns and:

- Tell God about something happy.
- Tell God what makes you feel sad.
- Tell God what you and your family need.
- Thank God for good gifts of home, friends, family, etc.

Treasure Nuggets from God's Word

"The Lord will hear me when I call
out to him."

Psalm 4:3

"Lord, even before I speak a word,
you know all about it."

Psalm 139:4

Prayer Starter

Dear God, I want to share my thoughts
and feelings with you. I am happy today
because _I am going_ . I am sad today because
_____. *to zoo*

3

How Should I Pray?

It doesn't matter "how" you pray. God just wants you to pray—any time, anywhere, and for any reason. Here are some ways people in the Bible prayed:

"Daniel knelt to pray by his open window."

Daniel 6:10

"David praised God as he danced for joy."

2 Samuel 6:14

"Elijah knelt on the ground with his head between his knees."

1 Kings 18:42

"Abraham fell with his face to the ground."

Genesis 17:3

"Solomon raised his hands in prayer."

1 Kings 8:22

"A leper knelt in front of Jesus."

Matthew 8:2

"Jesus looked up in the sky when he prayed at Lazarus' tomb."

John 11:41

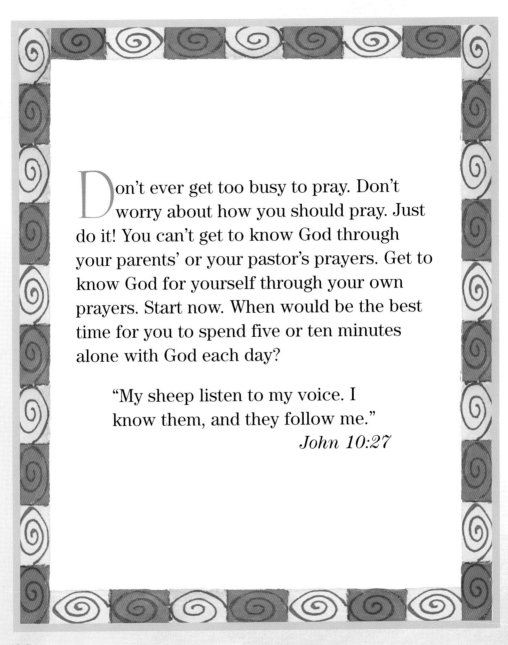

Don't ever get too busy to pray. Don't worry about how you should pray. Just do it! You can't get to know God through your parents' or your pastor's prayers. Get to know God for yourself through your own prayers. Start now. When would be the best time for you to spend five or ten minutes alone with God each day?

"My sheep listen to my voice. I know them, and they follow me."
John 10:27

God wants you to pray. So talk to God all day long—when you wake up, eat, do your chores, play, do schoolwork, or go to bed. Pray when you...

- Curl up in your favorite chair.
- Sit in a closet or kneel by your bed.
- Look out your window.
- Walk around the block. (This is a good time to pray for your neighbors.)

Stop Your Day! Let's Pray!

- First, read the Bible verses on the next page.

- Decide where and how you will pray. (Do something you've never done—like bow face down on the rug or lift your hands.)

- Before you pray, be calm and quiet. God is with you.

- Share with God what happened to you today.

Treasure Nuggets from God's Word

"Let us bow down and worship God.
Let us fall on our knees."

Psalm 95:6

"Lift up your hands . . . and praise
the Lord."

Psalm 134:2

"Sing for joy, even when [you]
are lying in bed."

Psalms 149:5

Prayer Starter

I bow my knees and lift my hands to you,
dear God. I want to thank you for the gifts
you've given me. Thank you for _My eathr_.

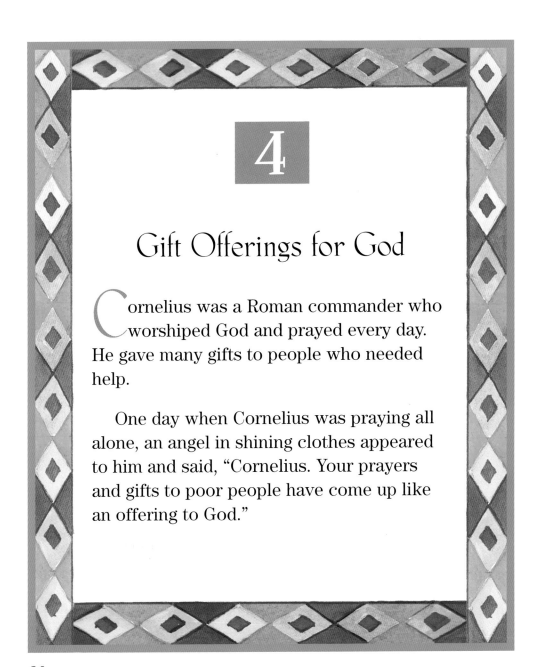

4

Gift Offerings for God

Cornelius was a Roman commander who worshiped God and prayed every day. He gave many gifts to people who needed help.

One day when Cornelius was praying all alone, an angel in shining clothes appeared to him and said, "Cornelius. Your prayers and gifts to poor people have come up like an offering to God."

The angel told Cornelius to send for Peter, a disciple of Jesus. When Peter came, he told Cornelius and his family about Jesus. While Peter was explaining how Jesus died on the cross and came alive again, the Holy Spirit suddenly came upon everyone who heard the message.

So Cornelius and his whole family believed in Jesus and were baptized.

The apostle John saw a vision of heaven. In his vision, an angel mixed sweet-smelling incense and the prayers of all God's people in a golden bowl.

Then the angel poured them on a golden altar in front of the throne of God. "The smoke of the incense together with the prayers of God's people . . . went up in front of God."

Revelation 8:3-4

When you pray, the words from your mind are like a sweet-smelling offering—a very special gift—to God. Just imagine! Your prayers and thanksgivings reach all the way up to God's throne in heaven.

In Psalm 141:2, David said, "Let my prayer come to you like the sweet smell of incense. When I lift up my hands in prayer, may it be like the evening sacrifice."

Time Alone With God

Jesus said, "When you pray, go into your room. Close the door and pray" (Matthew 6:6). It helps to have no distractions when you pray.

- Set a timer for five minutes.
- Go to your room and pray.
- Remember that your prayers are a gift offering to God.
- When the timer goes off, come back and read God's promises about prayer on the next page.

Treasure Nuggets from God's Word

"The prayers of God's people rose
up from the angel's hand. It went up
in front of God."

Revelation 8:4

"Lord, I will sacrifice a thank
offering to you. I will worship you."

Psalm 116:17

"The Lord's arm is not too weak to
save you. His ears aren't too deaf to
hear your cry for help."

Isaiah 59:1

Prayer Starter

Dear God, I am sending my prayers up to
your throne. I want to praise and thank you
today for _____.

5

Call for Your "Daddy"!

Prayer is like a small child reaching up to hold the hand of his strong father.

- God, our heavenly Father, is like a strong earthly father. But he is more loving and caring than the very best daddy in the whole world.

- All of us—kids, grownups, and grandparents—are holding our heavenly Father's hand when we pray.

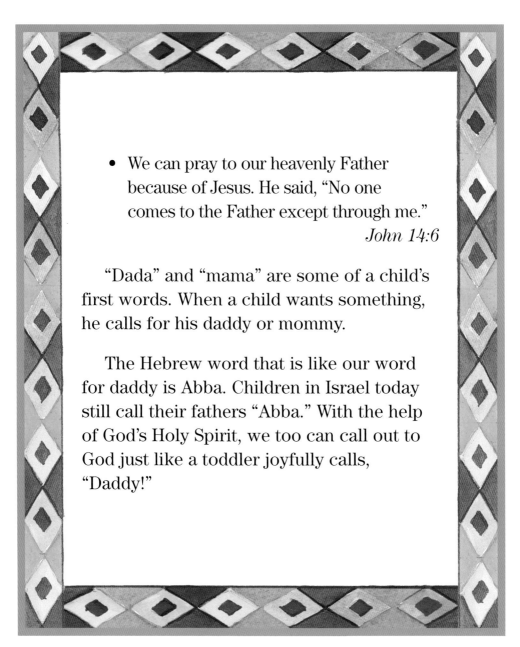

- We can pray to our heavenly Father because of Jesus. He said, "No one comes to the Father except through me."

  John 14:6

"Dada" and "mama" are some of a child's first words. When a child wants something, he calls for his daddy or mommy.

The Hebrew word that is like our word for daddy is Abba. Children in Israel today still call their fathers "Abba." With the help of God's Holy Spirit, we too can call out to God just like a toddler joyfully calls, "Daddy!"

Did Jesus Call God, "Daddy"?

When Jesus felt very sad and troubled before his arrest and crucifixion, he used the word "daddy" when he prayed to his Father in heaven.

In the Garden of Gethsemane, Jesus prayed, "Abba, everything is possible for you. Take this cup of suffering away from me. But let what you want be done, not what I want" (Mark 14:36).

Why Do We Call God
Our "Father"?

Do you know who told us to call God our "Father"? Jesus did. When the disciples asked Jesus to teach them to pray, he gave them a special prayer that we call "The Lord's Prayer."

Jesus said, "Your Father knows what you need even before you ask him. This is how you should pray. 'Our Father in heaven . . .'" (Matthew 6:8-9).

Child of the President

Think for a minute about the President of the United States. There is no way you can talk on the phone to the President. He is far too busy with the problems and decisions of running our country.

Secret Service agents stand by the doors leading to the President's office to keep visitors out. Only a few people get to see him. No one can go into his office without an invitation.

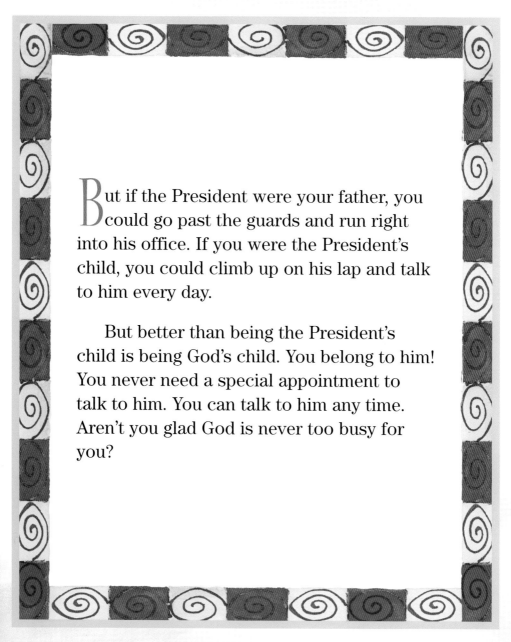

But if the President were your father, you could go past the guards and run right into his office. If you were the President's child, you could climb up on his lap and talk to him every day.

But better than being the President's child is being God's child. You belong to him! You never need a special appointment to talk to him. You can talk to him any time. Aren't you glad God is never too busy for you?

Open Your Heart in Prayer

Find a small box with a lid. Decorate with heart stickers or use markers to draw hearts on it.

- Read the Scriptures on the next page.
- Then sit very still. Hold the closed heart box in both hands.
- Search deep inside your heart for what you will say to God.
- Open your heart box and share the thoughts of your own heart with God.

Treasure Nuggets from God's Word

"Pray to your Father, who can't be seen."

Matthew 6:6

"Your Father knows what you need even before you ask him."

Matthew 6:8

Jesus said, "This is how you should pray. 'Our Father in heaven . . .'"

Matthew 6:9

Prayer Starter

Dear God, You're my Daddy and the best Father ever! You made me and you care for me. Please help me today with _____.

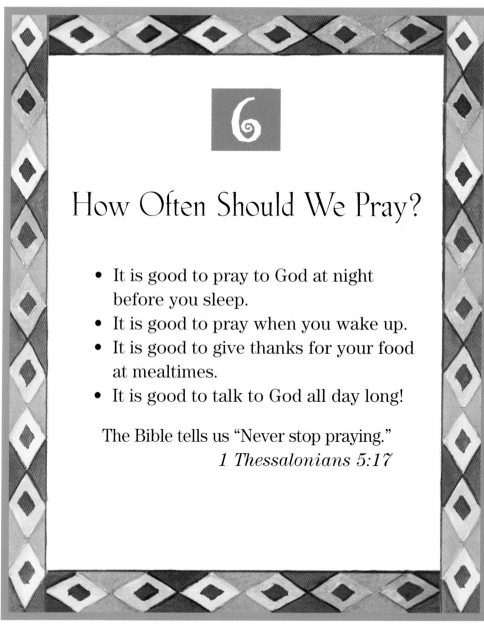

6

How Often Should We Pray?

- It is good to pray to God at night before you sleep.
- It is good to pray when you wake up.
- It is good to give thanks for your food at mealtimes.
- It is good to talk to God all day long!

The Bible tells us "Never stop praying."
1 Thessalonians 5:17

How Can I Pray All the Time?

Maybe you think it would be hard to pray at different times all during the day. But it isn't hard to talk all day to someone you love.

Remember that God is always with you. And God never gets tired of listening to you. Try talking with God all day—no matter where you are or what you are doing.

Daniel – a Man of Prayer

Daniel 6

Three times each day Daniel went into an upstairs room in his house. He opened the window and knelt down to pray. Then one day the king signed a new law that made it a crime for people to pray to anyone else except him.

Even then Daniel would not stop praying to God. And he still kept his window open when he prayed, even though he knew people would be watching him.

Some men saw Daniel pray. They told the king what Daniel did. So the king sent guards to arrest Daniel. For punishment, they threw him in a den of hungry lions. But God heard Daniel's prayers and sent an angel to protect him in the lions' den.

After the king set Daniel free, Daniel kept on praying. He often prayed for the people of Jerusalem. Once Daniel even prayed and fasted for 21 days—three long weeks (Daniel 9 and 10).

Prayer Rock Reminder

Find a smooth medium-sized rock, a 6-inch by 6-inch square of colorful fabric, a rubber band, and a 6-inch long ribbon.

To make your prayer rock reminder:

- Lay the rock on the center of the fabric (print side down).
- Pull the corners of the fabric up around rock to meet at top.
- Wind rubber band around "neck" of fabric.
- Tie a ribbon into a bow over the rubber band.

Place the prayer rock on your pillow each morning. At night before you lie down in bed, it will remind you to pray.

Treasure Nuggets from God's Word

"Never stop praying."

1 Thessalonians 5:17

"The followers of Jesus all came together regularly to pray."

Acts 1:14

"But I call out to God. And the Lord saves me. Evening, morning and noon I groan and cry out. And he hears my voice."

Psalm 55:16, 17

Prayer Starter

Dear God, I'm glad you never get tired of listening to me. I want to talk to you right now about _____.

7

Why Should We Thank and Praise God?

God is the great Creator of the world. Think about everything God has made. What are some good reasons to thank God?

- God's love lasts forever.
- God gave us amazing bodies and minds.
- God gives us many good things to enjoy.

"Give thanks to the Lord because he is good. His faithful love continues forever."

Psalm 106:1

We thank God for WHO he is—he is good. We thank God for his love—it never ends. We praise God when we sing to him and worship him.

Take time right now to tell God, "You are wonderful! You are awesome! You are good!"

King David said, "Who can praise God as much as he should be praised?"

Psalm 106:2

A Brave Choir

2 Chronicles 20:1-30

Long ago, three enemy armies came to fight King Jehosophat. The king called his people together and prayed, "Dear God, we don't know what to do, but we are looking to you to help us."

God said, "Do not be afraid . . . of this huge army. The battle is not yours. It is mine. Tomorrow march down against them . . . You will not have to fight this battle . . . I will save you."

Then everyone fell down and worshiped God while the singers stood and praised God with a very loud voice!

Early the next morning, the people came together again. Jehosophat asked some of the men to sing praises to God. The singers marched right in front of the army and praised God with their song, "Give thanks to the Lord. His faithful love continues forever."

And when the people began to sing and praise, God caused the three enemy armies to fight each other.

When the people of Judah arrived at the battlefield, they found that all the soldiers were destroyed. No one had escaped. And so the king and his people praised God again! He had saved them!

Will You Praise God At All Times?

- Will you trust God to hear every prayer and answer by giving his children what he thinks is best for them?

- Are you willing to praise God, even during hard times?

- Will you thank God like King Jehosophat and his people did—before you see answers to your prayers?

Praise God because nothing is impossible for him! Our Lord God is a powerful God who "is able to do far more than we could ever ask for or imagine."

Ephesians 3:20

A Thank–Bank of Praise

- Make a "Thank-Bank" by decorating an empty tin can or round container with pictures of things for which you are thankful. (Cut pictures out of magazines or draw pictures and tape them onto your container.)

- Cut strips of paper about 2 inches by 4 inches.

- Write (or have a grownup help you write) short prayers on these papers: Thank you, God, for my Daddy (sister, pet, family, and house).

- Take turns. Let each person pray and say thanks to God as he or she puts a prayer in the "Thank-Bank."

Treasure Nuggets from God's Word

"Let everything that has breath praise the Lord. Praise the Lord."
Psalm 150:6

"Give thanks no matter what happens. God wants you to thank him because you believe in Christ Jesus."
Psalm 92:1-2

"Shout to God with joy . . . Say to God, 'What wonderful things you do! Your power is so great.'"
Psalm 66:1-2

Prayer Starter

Dear God, I don't want to fuss or complain. Help me be thankful. I want to thank you today for these blessings _____.

8

Will You Cry for Help?

Have you ever heard an egg call for help? It happens. When a baby alligator has trouble breaking out of the egg as it hatches, it will cheep loudly to call for help.

As soon as the mother alligator hears her baby calling, she hurries to rescue it. She uses her teeth to help break open the hard shell so the baby is freed.

L ots of babies, both animal and human, cry when they need help. These cries usually bring their parents running! But it's not just babies who need help. Everybody needs help at one time or another. And who is the very BEST helper of all? God is.

Whenever we need help, God wants us to pray. The Bible tells us,

> "Are any of you in trouble? Then you should pray."
>
> *James 5:13*

Call for Help

God promised, "You will call out to me for help. And I will answer you" (Isaiah 58:9).

Many people call 911 on the telephone when they are in trouble. Sometimes they call a hospital or a doctor. It is good to call 911 or the doctor, but we also need to pray. If you pray, then it's God's job to answer your prayer.

Long ago God answered Elisha's prayers when the King of Aram sent his army to surround the city where Elisha lived.

Elisha's servant was afraid when he saw all the soldiers. So Elisha told him, "Don't be afraid. Those who are with us are more than those who are with them." And Elisha prayed, "Lord, open my servant's eyes so he can see."

God answered Elisha's prayer and the servant saw a heavenly army of fiery horses and chariots surrounding the enemy army. Then Elisha prayed again, "Lord, make these soldiers blind." And God did it! The soldiers could not capture Elisha (2 Kings 6:8-23).

Newspaper Prayer

- Read the scriptures on the next page.
- Look for newspapers (or magazines) that tell about reports of problems and situations where God's help is needed.
- Look for some reports with photos.
- Select a specific problem or person to pray for.
- Then pray about the problem or situation you have chosen.

Treasure Nuggets from God's Word

"Trust in God at all times . . . Tell him all of your troubles. God is our place of safety."

Psalms 62:8

"The Lord is ready to help all those who call out to him. He helps those who really mean it when they call out to him . . . He hears their cry and saves them."

Psalm 145:18-19

Prayer Starter

A lot of people need your help, dear God. Please be with those who are sad and who suffer. And especially take care of these people I love <u>My famliy</u>.

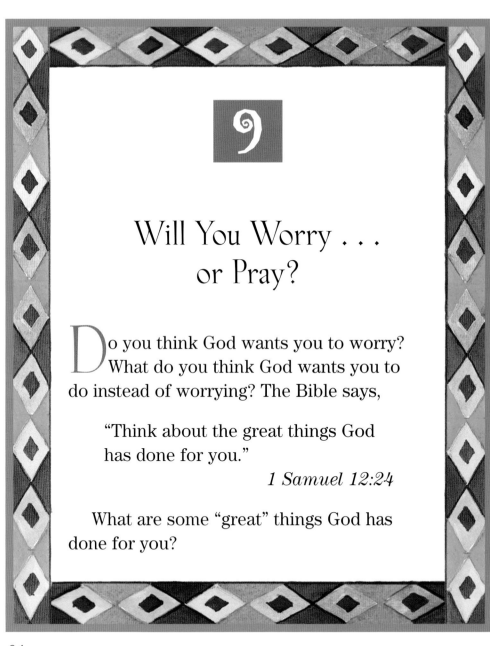

9

Will You Worry . . . or Pray?

Do you think God wants you to worry? What do you think God wants you to do instead of worrying? The Bible says,

> "Think about the great things God has done for you."
>
> *1 Samuel 12:24*

What are some "great" things God has done for you?

King David wrote this prayer: "Our people of long ago put their trust in you . . . they cried out to you and were saved."

- Who are some people God helped long ago in the Bible?
- How has God helped your family in the past?
- How can you be sure God will help you in the future?
- Will you pray and thank God when you face troubles today?

"They trusted in you, and you didn't let them down."
Psalm 22:4-5

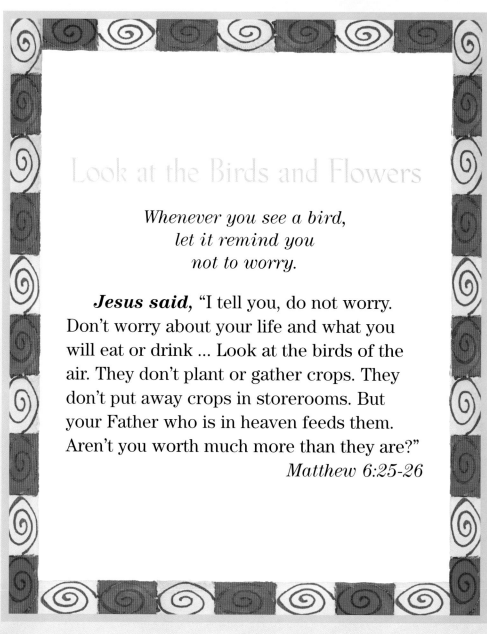

Look at the Birds and Flowers

Whenever you see a bird,
let it remind you
not to worry.

Jesus said, "I tell you, do not worry. Don't worry about your life and what you will eat or drink ... Look at the birds of the air. They don't plant or gather crops. They don't put away crops in storerooms. But your Father who is in heaven feeds them. Aren't you worth much more than they are?"

Matthew 6:25-26

Jesus also said, "And don't worry about your body and what you will wear . . . See how the wild flowers grow. They don't work or make clothing. But here is what I tell you. Not even Solomon in all of his glory was dressed like one of those flowers."

Matthew 6:25, 28-29

What do you worry about the most? If God cares for every daffodil and dandelion, won't he take good care of you? Put all your worries into God's hands.

"Palms Up, Palms Down"

- Hold your hands out with your palms up. Pretend to put all your worries in your out-stretched palms. Then give them to God. Just let them go.

- Tell God, "I'm handing all my troubles to you. Please take care of them. And help me not to worry."

- Now turn your palms down. Imagine you are dropping all your worries into God's hands.

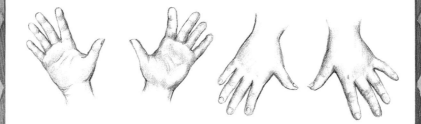

68

Treasure Nuggets from God's Word

Jesus said, "Don't worry . . . Don't worry about tomorrow."

Matthew 6:31, 34

"Don't worry about anything. Instead, tell God about everything. Ask and pray."

Philippians 4:6

Jesus said, "Come to me, all of you who are tired and are carrying heavy loads. I will give you rest."

Matthew 11:28

Prayer Starter

Thanks for all the ways you take care of me, dear God. I want to give my worries to you. Some of my worries are _____.

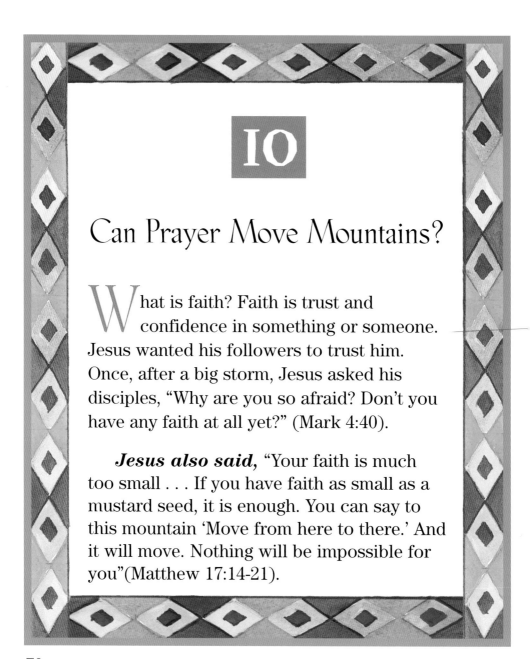

10

Can Prayer Move Mountains?

What is faith? Faith is trust and confidence in something or someone. Jesus wanted his followers to trust him. Once, after a big storm, Jesus asked his disciples, "Why are you so afraid? Don't you have any faith at all yet?" (Mark 4:40).

Jesus also said, "Your faith is much too small . . . If you have faith as small as a mustard seed, it is enough. You can say to this mountain 'Move from here to there.' And it will move. Nothing will be impossible for you"(Matthew 17:14-21).

We all have "mountains" of troubles in our lives. But do we all have "seeds" of faith? Do you expect God to answer your prayer?

Jesus said again, "Have faith in God . . . Suppose one of you says to this mountain, 'Go and throw yourself into the sea.' You must not doubt in your heart. You must believe that what you say will happen. Then it will be done for you. So I tell you, when you pray for something, believe that you have already received it. Then it will be yours."

Mark 11:22-24

71

No Faith

When people didn't have faith, Jesus couldn't do as many miracles. This happened in Jesus' hometown. The people of Nazareth had known Jesus from the time he was a little boy. They didn't believe he was the Son of God.

Later, when Jesus came back to Nazareth, he "laid his hands on a few sick people and healed them. But he could not do any other miracles there. He was amazed because they had no faith" (Mark 6:5-6).

Do You Pray with "Faith"?

Because God keeps every promise, we can trust him. The Bible says, "God will remain faithful" (1 Timothy 2:13).

- Don't trust in good luck charms, four-leaf clovers, lucky horseshoes, or anything else—only trust in God.
- Don't doubt and say, "I hope God will hear my prayer."
- Have a sure faith that says, "God will hear me and help me."

A Great Prayer of Faith
1 Kings 18

The prophet Elijah knew that God answered prayer. So Elijah set up a contest with 450 prophets of the Baal-god to prove who was the real God.

All morning and afternoon the followers of Baal called to their god. They shouted. They danced around their altar. They even cut themselves with swords. But Baal never answered their prayers.

Finally it was Elijah's turn to pray. First Elijah built an altar of stones and dug a big ditch around it. After he set out wood for the fire, he cut up a bull for a sacrifice and placed it on the wood. Then twelve large jars of water were poured over the altar until everything was soaking wet.

Now Elijah prayed one short prayer. He asked God to send fire to burn up the offering.

Elijah prayed, "Lord . . . Today let everyone know that you are God in Israel . . . Lord, answer me. Then these people will know that you are the one and only God."

Immediately, fire fell from heaven. It burnt everything—the bull, the wood, the altar stones, and it even licked up all the water in the ditch! When the people who were watching saw this, they fell flat on their faces and cried out, "The Lord is the one and only God!" Finally, they believed!

What About Your Faith?

When you say "Amen" at the end of your prayer, it doesn't mean "the end." Amen means, "Let it be so!" It means that you believe God will do what is exactly the best. What are some good reasons why you can trust God to do the impossible?

- God can do anything!
- God is bigger than any problem. "Nothing is impossible with God."

Luke 1:37

Will You Trust?

- Talk with your parents about how the
  following actions require faith.
    Sitting in a chair.
    Riding in a car.
    Flying in an airplane.
- Have your parent read the "Faith Chapter"
  (Hebrews 11:1-13) to you.

Treasure Nuggets From God's Word

"When you pray, you must believe. You must not doubt."

James 1:6

"Without faith it isn't possible to please God."

Hebrews 11:6

"When you pray for something, believe that you have already received it. Then it will be yours."

Mark 11:24

Prayer Starter

Dear God, help me trust you like Elijah did. I know you can do anything. Here's where I need your help today _____.

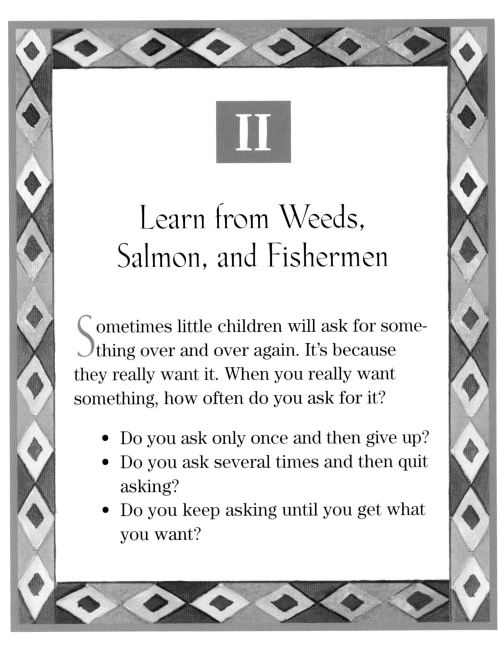

II

Learn from Weeds, Salmon, and Fishermen

Sometimes little children will ask for some-thing over and over again. It's because they really want it. When you really want something, how often do you ask for it?

- Do you ask only once and then give up?
- Do you ask several times and then quit asking?
- Do you keep asking until you get what you want?

The word "ask" in the Bible means to ask more than once, to be persistent. It means to keep on asking without giving up.

Jesus said, "Ask [and keep on asking], and it will be given to you. Search, and you will find. Knock, and the door will be opened to you. Everyone who asks [keeps on asking] will receive. He who searches will find. The door will be opened to the one who knocks" (Matthew 7:7-8).

Learn to Be Persistent!

- Thistles and dandelions send out lots of seeds to make more plants. It is impossible to get rid of these pesky weeds because they keep coming up!

- Salmon swim hundreds of miles upstream to lay their eggs. And when they are going upstream, they don't stop. They just keep going and going until they reach the place where they were born.

- Even a good fisherman doesn't always catch a fish. But a good fisherman never gives up trying! He keeps going back to the river or lake to fish some more.

A Persistent Friend

Luke 11:5, 8

Jesus told this story to encourage us to keep on praying: "Suppose someone goes to his friend at midnight. He says, 'Friend, lend me three loaves of bread. A friend of mine on a journey has come to stay with me. I have nothing for him to eat.'

"That person will not get up. And he won't give the man bread just because he is his friend. But because the man keeps on asking, he will get up and give him as much as he needs."

Elijah Didn't Quit

1 Kings 18:41-46

"Elijah was just like us. He prayed hard that it wouldn't rain. And it didn't rain on the land for three and a half years. Then he prayed again."

James 5:17-18

He prayed once and nothing happened. Then he prayed five more times. Still nothing happened. But the seventh time Elijah prayed, a small cloud appeared in the sky. Then Elijah knew—rain was on its way. And God sent a downpour of rain to water the land.

A Persistent Widow

Luke 18:1-8

Once Jesus told his disciples a story to show them that they should always pray and never give up.

Jesus said, "In a certain town there was a judge. He didn't have any respect for God or care about people. A widow in that town came to the judge again and again. She kept begging him, 'Make things right for me. Someone is doing me wrong'".

Jesus said, "For some time the judge refused. But finally he said to himself, 'I don't have any respect for God. I don't care about people. But this widow keeps bothering me. So I will see that things are made right for her. If I don't, she will wear me out by coming again and again!'"

Then Jesus said, "God's chosen people cry out to him day and night. Won't he make things right for them? Will he keep putting them off? I tell you, God will see that things are made right for them. He will make sure it happens quickly."

What do you think would have happened if the widow had stopped asking the judge to help her?

What about you? Will you be persistent when you pray? God wants to give you good gifts. Don't give up asking God to help you and to help others.

Let Your Faith Rise Up

Jesus said, "In this world you will have trouble. But cheer up! I have won the battle over the world" (John 16:33).

Let your faith rise above every problem.

- Place a large walnut in a glass quart jar. (The walnut stands for a Christian.)
- Name a problem of life, like sickness, an accident, or a flood.
- At the same time, pour a handful of dried beans on top of the nut.
- Shake the jar after adding the beans (Walnut will rise to the top.)

Treasure Nuggets from God's Word

"When you pray, be faithful (don't give up!)"

Romans 12:12

"God will see that things are made right for his people."

Luke 18:8

"The prayer of a godly person is powerful. It makes things happen."

James 5:16

Prayer Starter

Dear God, I've prayed a long time about some things. I want to talk to you about them again today. Please hear my prayers about _____.

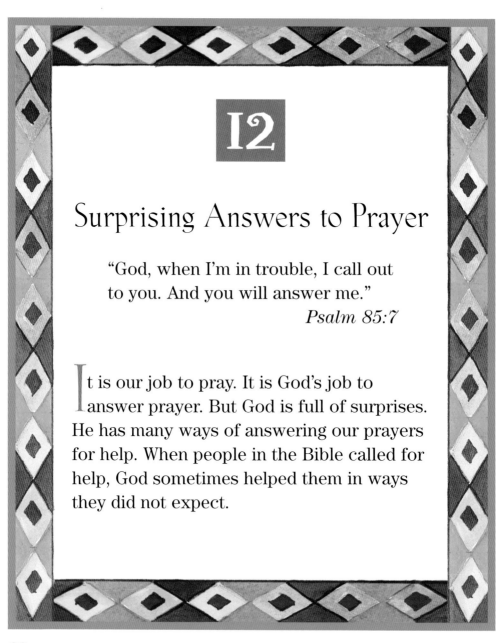

12

Surprising Answers to Prayer

"God, when I'm in trouble, I call out
to you. And you will answer me."

Psalm 85:7

It is our job to pray. It is God's job to answer prayer. But God is full of surprises. He has many ways of answering our prayers for help. When people in the Bible called for help, God sometimes helped them in ways they did not expect.

Help in the Belly of A Fish

Jonah 2:1-10

Jonah prayed after a big fish swallowed him. He said, "When I had almost drowned, I called for help. And you listened to my cry . . .When my life was nearly over, I remembered you, Lord. My prayer rose up to you. It reached you in your holy temple in heaven . . . I will sing a song of thanks . . . Lord, you are the one who saves."

Then God gave the fish a command. And the fish spit Jonah onto dry land!

Help for A Desperate Widow

2 Kings 4:1-7

A widow came to Elisha and said, "My husband is dead. You know how much respect he had for the Lord. But he owed money to someone. And now that person is coming to take my two boys away. They will become his slaves."

Elisha wanted to help. He asked her, "What do you have in your house?"

"I don't have anything there," she said. "All I have is a little olive oil."

92

Elisha said, "Ask all of your neighbors for empty jars. Get as many jars as you can. Then go inside your house. Shut the door behind you and your sons. Pour oil into all the jars."

The widow obeyed. Her sons handed empty jars to her as she poured oil from her little bottle. When all of the jars were full, the oil stopped flowing! What an amazing gift! She sold the oil and paid off her debt. Now her sons didn't have to be slaves. And they lived on the money that was left.

Help in A Terrible Storm

Matthew 8:23-27

Once when Jesus slept in a boat, a terrible storm came up on the lake. The waves crashed over the boat. The terrified disciples woke Jesus and said, "Lord! Save us! We're going to drown!"

Jesus said, "Your faith is so small! Why are you so afraid?" Then Jesus stood up and ordered the winds and the waves to stop. Instantly the winds and the waves became calm. What a surprise!

Help in Prison

Acts 16:16-40

Once Paul and Silas were whipped and thrown in prison for doing something good. Instead of complaining, they prayed and sang praise to God.

Suddenly, at midnight, God sent a powerful earthquake. "It shook the prison from top to bottom. All at once the prison doors flew open. Everybody's chains came loose." And God used this surprise answer to change the lives of the jailer and his family and to release Paul and Silas from prison.

95

My Thankful Book

Never take God's love or his help for granted. Be thankful for all the ways God answers your prayers.

- Give each person several pieces of plain paper for the inside pages of their book.
- Use two sheets of construction paper for front and back covers.
- Draw pictures of your troubles.
- Draw pictures of the many ways God helped you and your family. (Leave a few blank pages at the end so you can add to the book later.
- Punch holes along left edges and tie your book together with yarn.

I am thankful because I feel safe in my house.

Treasure Nuggets from God's Word

God says, "Call out to me when trouble comes. I will save you. And you will honor me."

Psalm 50:15

"God, save me. My troubles are like a flood. I'm up to my neck in them."

Psalm 59:1

"Lord, answer me because your love is so good . . . Answer me quickly. I'm in trouble."

Psalm 69:16-17

Prayer Starter

Help me, dear God. And help my family during times of trouble. I know you will answer my prayers and help us with _____.

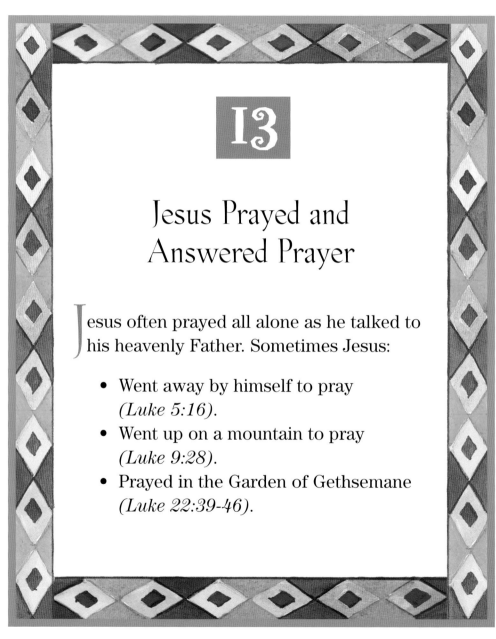

13

Jesus Prayed and Answered Prayer

Jesus often prayed all alone as he talked to his heavenly Father. Sometimes Jesus:

- Went away by himself to pray *(Luke 5:16)*.
- Went up on a mountain to pray *(Luke 9:28)*.
- Prayed in the Garden of Gethsemane *(Luke 22:39-46)*.

Jesus also prayed when he was with other people:

- He gave thanks before he fed over 5,000 people *(Luke 9:16).*
- He thanked God before he raised Lazarus *(John 11:41-42).*
- He gave thanks at the Last Supper *(Matthew 26:26-27).*
- He prayed while he hung on the cross *(Matthew 27:46, Luke 23:34, 46).*
- He blessed bread and then disappeared *(Luke 24:30-31).*
- He blessed his disciples before going up into heaven *(Luke 24:50-51).*

When Did Jesus Pray for You?

In the Garden of Gethsemane before he died on the cross, Jesus prayed for his disciples and for you.

He prayed, "Father, I am praying for all those you have given me . . . I do not pray that you will take them out of the world. I pray that you will keep them safe from the evil one . . . I pray also for those who will believe in me because of their message. Father, I pray that all of them will be one" (John 17:9, 15, 20-21).

Jesus Still Prays for You

Do you know that Jesus is still praying for you and me?

The Bible tells us, "Christ Jesus is at the right hand of God and is also praying for us" (Romans 8:34).

What do you think Jesus is praying for you?

> "People now come to God through Jesus. And he is able to save them completely . . . Jesus lives forever. He prays for them."
>
> *Hebrews 7:25*

Jesus Helped People When Others Prayed

- A father brought his demon-possessed son to Jesus (Mark 9:14-29).
- A royal official asked Jesus to heal his dying son (John 4:46-54).
- Jarius asked Jesus to heal his daughter (Luke 8:41-56).
- A foreign woman asked Jesus to heal her daughter (Matthew 15:21-28).
- A Roman soldier prayed for his ill servant (Matthew 8:5-13).
- Several men brought a paralyzed friend to Jesus (Matthew 9:1-8).

Who Will You
Bring to Jesus in Prayer?

"At sunset, people brought to Jesus all who were
sick. He placed his hands on each one and healed
them" (Luke 4:40). Just like people brought their loved
ones to Jesus, you too can "carry" other people to
Jesus in prayer.

- What about your family? Does anyone need
  prayer?
- What about your relatives? Who needs prayer?
- What about those who live nearby? Do they need
  prayer?

Don't Forget to Pray!

When Samuel was God's prophet, he never stopped praying for the people of Israel. He told them, "I would never sin against the Lord by failing to pray for you" (1 Samuel 12:23).

Did you know God wants you to pray for other people? The Bible says, "Pray for one another" (James 5:16).

Make a prayer list of people whom you will bring to Jesus in prayer.

Will You Pray for People to Work in God's Kingdom?

Jesus loved and cared for the crowds who followed him. He said that all the people were like a big field of ripe wheat ready to be harvested. And he wanted his disciples to pray for more workers.

Jesus told his disciples, "The harvest is huge. But there are only a few workers. So ask the Lord of the harvest to send workers out into his harvest field" (Matthew 9:37-38).

Adopt A Country

Jesus said, "Go and make disciples of all nations" (Matthew 28:19). One way you can do that is by prayer! When you pray for people, Jesus will touch them. And you become a helper in God's kingdom.

- Choose a country to pray for this week.
- Look up information about the country.
- Fix a typical meal eaten in the country. (Ask your mom to help you find recipes for the country you have chosen.)
- Before you eat, pray for the country, its leaders and people.

Treasure Nuggets from God's Word

"Always keep on praying for all of God's people."

Ephesians 6:18

"Pray for everyone. Ask God to bless them. Give thanks for them."

1 Timothy 2:1

"Pray for kings. Pray for all who are in authority . . . That is good. It pleases God our Savior."

1 Timothy 2:2-4

Prayer Starter

Dear Jesus, I'm glad you pray for me. Please hear my prayers for other people and other countries right now, especially for

_____.

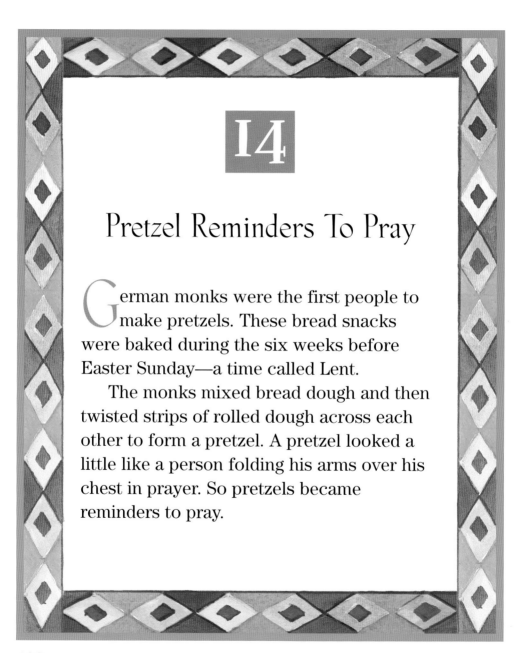

14

Pretzel Reminders To Pray

German monks were the first people to make pretzels. These bread snacks were baked during the six weeks before Easter Sunday—a time called Lent.

The monks mixed bread dough and then twisted strips of rolled dough across each other to form a pretzel. A pretzel looked a little like a person folding his arms over his chest in prayer. So pretzels became reminders to pray.

The cross shape in the pretzel also reminded people that we can pray to God because Jesus died for us on the cross. Take a minute now and fold your arms across each other on your chest. Remember how Jesus helps you pray.

> "Through faith in Christ we can approach God. We can come to God freely. We can come without fear."
>
> *Ephesians 3:12*

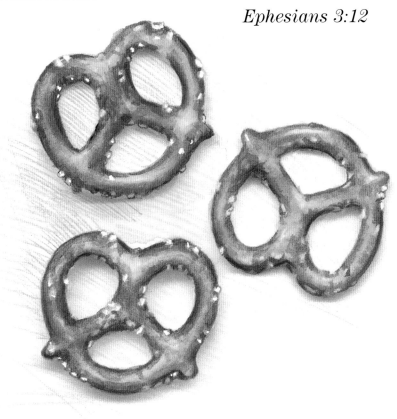

When you bake or cook, you need to follow the recipe's directions. When you pray, you need to follow God's "directions."

Jesus said, "Ask for anything in my name."
John 14:14

What does it mean to pray in Jesus' name? It means that Jesus is the reason we can pray to God! He is "the way" to God.

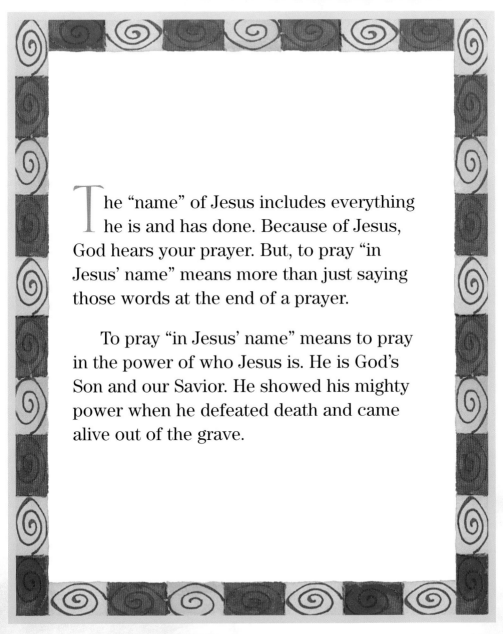

The "name" of Jesus includes everything he is and has done. Because of Jesus, God hears your prayer. But, to pray "in Jesus' name" means more than just saying those words at the end of a prayer.

To pray "in Jesus' name" means to pray in the power of who Jesus is. He is God's Son and our Savior. He showed his mighty power when he defeated death and came alive out of the grave.

Pretzel Prayers

- Get a bag of pretzels. See how they are twisted to look like arms folded across someone's chest.
- Place your arms across your chest in the shape of an 'X' (a cross).
- Take turns praying "in Jesus' Name." Remember that he gave his life for you.
- At the end of your prayer time, use your finger to trace a cross on your forehead as a reminder that you belong to Jesus.
- Enjoy eating the pretzels!

Treasure Nuggets from God's Word

Jesus promised, "You may ask for anything in my name."

John 14:14

Jesus promised, "I will do anything you ask in my name."

John 14:13

Jesus said, "If you remain joined to me and my words remain in you, ask for anything you wish. And it will be given to you."

John 15:7

Prayer Starter

Dear God, I come to you because Jesus gave his life for me. Now I want to ask you some special requests in his name _____.

15

Pray By Yourself?
Pray With Others?

Most of the time we pray by ourselves. But praying with other people is also important. Jesus wanted his disciples to agree together in prayer. He said, "Suppose two of you on earth agree about anything you ask for. My Father in heaven will do it for you" (Matthew 18:19).

- Do you pray with other family members in your home?
- Where else do you pray with people?

Prayer Meeting Surprise!

Acts 12:4-19

After Jesus went into heaven, his followers continued to pray together. They also told many people about Jesus. King Herod tried to stop them. He arrested Peter and put him in prison. Sixteen soldiers were assigned to guard Peter.

The Christians knew King Herod planned to put Peter on trial and then kill him. While Peter was kept in prison, the Christians prayed day and night for him.

God heard their prayers and sent an angel to Peter's prison cell. The angel woke Peter and said, "Get up!" Peter had been chained to two guards, but as he got up the chains fell off his wrists.

The angel led Peter past all the sleeping guards. When they got to the main prison gate, it opened by itself. Peter followed the angel down the street. Suddenly the angel disappeared.

Peter hurried to the home where many people were praying all night for him. When he knocked on the door, a servant girl answered. She recognized Peter's voice and ran to tell the others that Peter was at the door. But no one believed her.

Peter continued to knock. Some of the men went to answer the door and discovered—it was Peter! God had answered their prayers and saved Peter from death!

Pray Alone

Long ago, religious people stood on street corners and prayed in public. They said their prayers loudly to impress other people.

Jesus doesn't want us to show off or brag when we pray. He said, "When you pray, go into your room. Close the door and pray to your Father, who can't be seen. He will reward you. Your Father sees what is done secretly" (Matthew 6:6).

Find a good time and place for you to have a "secret" time alone with God:

- Without distraction of radio, stereo, or television.
- When you won't be interrupted.
- When you're wide awake (so you won't fall asleep).

Paper Chain Prayers

- Read the Scriptures on the next page.
- Cut out twelve strips of construction paper about one-inch wide by nine-inches long.
- Write a prayer request on each strip. Pray your requests out loud.
- Make a paper chain from all the paper strips.
- Hang the chain by your kitchen table, or your bed, or on a mirror to help you remember your prayers the next time you pray.

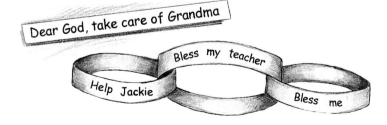

Dear God, take care of Grandma

Bless my teacher

Help Jackie

Bless me

Treasure Nuggets from God's Word

"When you pray, go into your room. Close the door."

Matthew 6:6

Jesus said, "Where two or three people meet together in my name, I am there with them."

Matthew 18:20

Jesus said, "Suppose two of you on earth agree about anything you ask for. My Father in heaven will do it for you."

Matthew 18:19

Prayer Starter

Dear God, thank you for being here with us when we pray. We know you will hear us as we pray together for _____.

16

Be God's "Fire Extinguisher"

Do you have a fire extinguisher at your house? Everyone needs a fire extinguisher when fire breaks out!

When troubles happen, God wants to use you as his "fire extinguisher." God puts you in the right place at the right time! You don't need to go find someone else to pray when there is an emergency. As part of God's Emergency Prayer Team, you can pray anytime and anyplace.

"God is able to do far more than we could ever ask for or imagine."

Ephesians 3:20

It will make a difference if you STOP and pray when:

- You see someone in trouble.
- You hear news reports about disasters.
- You are around kids who make bad choices.

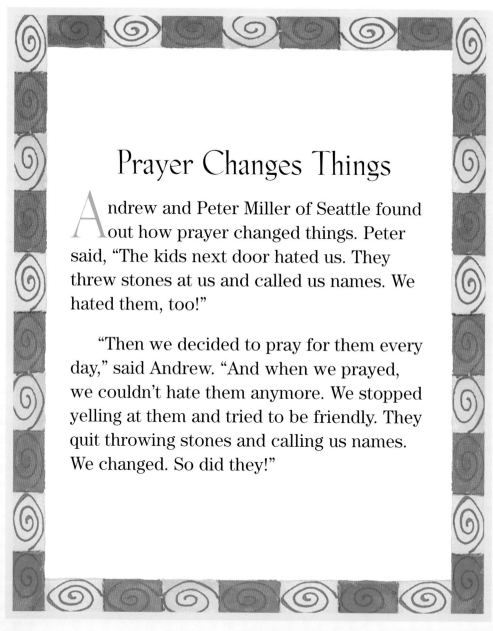

Prayer Changes Things

Andrew and Peter Miller of Seattle found out how prayer changed things. Peter said, "The kids next door hated us. They threw stones at us and called us names. We hated them, too!"

"Then we decided to pray for them every day," said Andrew. "And when we prayed, we couldn't hate them anymore. We stopped yelling at them and tried to be friendly. They quit throwing stones and calling us names. We changed. So did they!"

Moses Prayed

Exodus 32:1-14, 34:1-8

Once, out in the wilderness, the people of Israel made a golden calf. They bowed down and worshiped it, even though God had forbidden them to have any other gods.

So Moses asked God to forgive them. He prayed, "Please take pity on your people. Don't destroy them!" Because of Moses' prayer, God forgave the people. And God helped Moses lead them to the Promised Land.

125

Moses Prayed for His Brother and Sister

Numbers 12:1-15

Once Miriam and Aaron said bad things about their brother Moses. They criticized him because he married a foreign woman. But their talk made God angry. God told them, "With Moses I speak face to face . . . So why were you not afraid to speak against my servant Moses?"

Suddenly Miriam's skin turned white as snow—she became a leper! Now she would have to leave her family and move far away so they would not catch her skin disease.

Aaron felt sorry for what he and his sister had done. He told Moses, "We have committed a very foolish sin. Please don't hold it against us."

So Moses forgave Aaron and Miriam for talking against him. And Moses went to God and prayed, "Please heal my sister!" Immediately, because Moses prayed, God completely healed Miriam.

Share with each other a time when someone talked about you? Then think if others have criticized you or treated you unfairly?

- Will you forgive those who talk against you?
- Will you pray for people who make fun of you?
- Will you pray for people who get into trouble and who break God's commandments?

Be God's fire extinguisher. Make a big difference in the lives of people who hurt you and who are mean to others. Do what Jesus said:

"Love your enemies. Do good to those who hate you. Bless those who call down curses on you. And pray for those who treat you badly."

Luke 6:27-28

A Handful of Prayer

Use the fingers on your hand to pray:

- THUMB – pray for people who live in your home.

- POINTER FINGER – pray for cousins, grandparents, aunts, and uncles.

- TALLEST FINGER – pray for neighbors, the mailman, a grocery store clerk, and friends.

- FOURTH FINGER – pray for teachers, leaders, and the head of your country.

- LITTLE FINGER – pray for yourself!

Treasure Nuggets from God's Word

"This is how you should pray . . .
'Forgive us our sins, just as we also
have forgiven those who sin against
us.'"

Matthew 6:9, 12

"Don't pay back evil with evil. Don't
pay back unkind words with unkind
words. Instead, pay them back with
kind words (prayers!)"

1 Peter 3:9

Prayer Starter

Dear God, some angry people want to
hurt our leaders and our country. Please
change the hearts of all our enemies,
especially _____.

What Do Penguins Teach Us About Prayer?

Emperor Penguins live in a cold icy world. The mother penguin lays an egg at the beginning of winter. Then she leaves to go feed in the ocean.

Because there are no materials to build a nest, the daddy penguin provides a "nest" for his baby. He rolls the egg-baby on top of his feet so it won't freeze on the ice. God gave the father penguin a special fold of skin to hang down and cover the egg like a warm blanket.

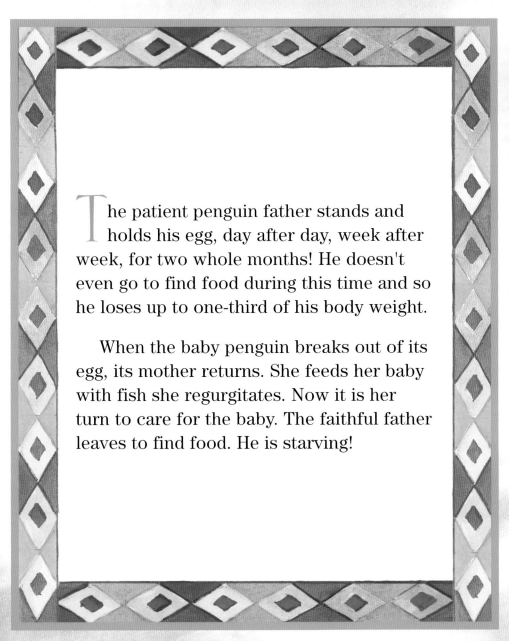

The patient penguin father stands and holds his egg, day after day, week after week, for two whole months! He doesn't even go to find food during this time and so he loses up to one-third of his body weight.

When the baby penguin breaks out of its egg, its mother returns. She feeds her baby with fish she regurgitates. Now it is her turn to care for the baby. The faithful father leaves to find food. He is starving!

Are You Patient . . . or Impatient?

"Be still. Be patient. Wait for the Lord to act."

Psalm 37:7

What can you learn from Emperor penguins? Someday you may need to be patient and keep praying when you feel like giving up because nothing seems to be happening. Instead of complaining about your prayers not being answered, will you patiently wait for your prayers to "hatch"?

Don't Give Up Praying

WAIT patiently for God's answer when you pray.

- Don't give up because something looks impossible.
- Don't give up because something seems too hard.
- Don't be lazy or too busy to keep on praying.
- Don't think God isn't listening.

A Mother Who Didn't Give Up

Matthew 15:21-28

Once when Jesus and his disciples were walking, a woman from another country followed behind them. She begged Jesus to help her daughter who was suffering.

At first Jesus ignored the woman. But she wouldn't leave even when the disciples told Jesus, "Tell the woman to go away. She keeps following us and shouting for you to help."

Jesus never said a word. He just kept walking.

The woman kept begging Jesus to help her daughter.

Finally Jesus turned to her and said, "Woman, you have great faith! I will do what you asked me to do." And at that moment her daughter was completely healed!

- What if the woman had given up after asking once?
- What can you learn from this woman's example?

Table Reminder

- Give each person a regular sheet of heavy paper.
- Fold paper in half so it sits on the table like a "tent" on the table.
- Write down (or draw pictures of) something or someone you or your family have prayed about for a long time.
- Write a promise of God about prayer on the paper.
- Use your table tent at each meal as you keep on praying.

Wait for the Lord.

Heal Grandpa

Treasure Nuggets from God's Word

"Wait for the Lord. Be strong and don't lose hope."

Psalm 27:14

"Be strong, all of you who put your hope in the Lord. Never give up."

Psalm 31:24

"Be still. Be patient. Wait for the Lord to act."

Psalm 37:7

Prayer Starter

Dear God, I know you hear me. I don't want to ever stop talking to you. Help me be patient as I pray about _____.

18

"Seed", "Arrow", and "Popcorn" Prayers

What good is one small seed? Well, one apple seed could grow into one apple tree. And each apple usually has five seeds. If a tree had ten apples that would make 50 seeds, and those 50 seeds could make 50 more trees! If a tree produced 100 apples, then 500 more apple trees could be planted.

Only God knows how many apples can come from just one seed you plant!

It is the same with one small prayer. Every time you pray for someone, it is like planting a "seed-prayer." You can be sure every seed-prayer will bring forth a great harvest.

Think of a one-seed prayer to pray for one other person. When God works through your prayer in that person's life, many other people could be helped. It might be hundreds! Even thousands!

Arrow Prayers

Just like archers shoot their arrows at a target, you can send out your arrow-prayers at living targets:

- For a baby who is crying.
- For someone who looks sad.
- For your mom when she feels discouraged.
- For a busy grocery store checker.

Popcorn Prayers

Just like small kernels of corn explode when heated in a hot air popper, so a prayer can pop or burst out of our mouths at anytime! So when problems come, take time for a quick prayer!

- When you see an accident.
- When a house is on fire.
- When a storm heads your way.
- When fights and arguments begin.

Pray for Your City

- Pin a map of your city on the wall.
- Close your eyes. Stretch out your finger and touch the map.
- Open your eyes. See where your finger is. Pray for the people who live there.
- Then pray for the homes and families on your "block."
- Now thank God that he will answer your prayers. (But you may have to wait until you get to heaven to find out what happened when you prayed!)

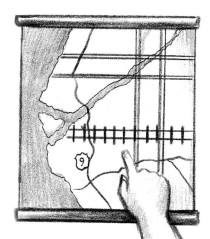

Treasure Nuggets from God's Word

"Pray for one another."

James 5:16

"Pray that we will live peaceful and quiet lives. And pray that we will be godly and holy."

1 Timothy 2:2

God said, "I tried to find someone who would pray to me for the land [and people.]"

Ezekiel 22:30

Prayer Starter

Dear God, please take care of the people who need you right now. I pray you will expecially take care of _____.

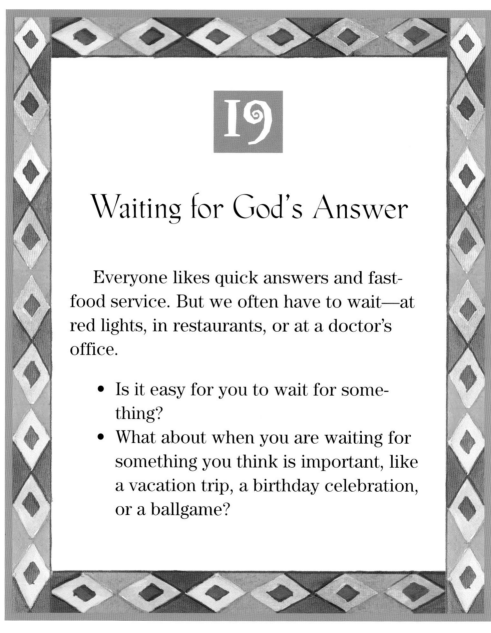

19

Waiting for God's Answer

Everyone likes quick answers and fast-food service. But we often have to wait—at red lights, in restaurants, or at a doctor's office.

- Is it easy for you to wait for something?
- What about when you are waiting for something you think is important, like a vacation trip, a birthday celebration, or a ballgame?

When Have You Waited?

- When have you waited for God to answer your prayer?
- What is the longest time you have prayed for something to happen?
- Why do you think God waits to answer your prayers?
- Why do you need patience when you pray?

Who Waited for God to Answer?

1 Kings 18:36-46

Remember how Elijah and the prophets of Baal had a contest to see which of their gods was the true God. The prophets of Baal prayed all day. Their god never answered. But when Elijah prayed, God answered immediately with fire from heaven!

But then, soon afterwards, Elijah prayed for rain and God did not answer. So Elijah prayed again. Still no answer. Elijah prayed again, again, again, again, and again. Finally, after seven prayers, God sent a downpour of rain.

- Abraham waited 25 years for the son God promised (Genesis 12-17).
- Joseph waited many years in prison (Genesis 39:19 - 41:43).
- Zechariah and his wife prayed and waited for a baby. When they were too old to have children, an angel told Zechariah, "Your prayer has been heard. Your wife Elizabeth will have a child" (Luke 1:13-14).
- The disciples prayed and waited ten days for the Holy Spirit (Acts 1:4-5).

An Urgent Request

John 11

Mary and Martha sent word to Jesus that their brother Lazarus was very ill. Jesus received their message, but he did not go to their home in the town of Bethany. Finally, when Jesus knew Lazarus was dead, he went to Bethany.

When Jesus arrived at their town, Martha ran out to meet him. She said, "Lord, if you had been here, my brother would not have died."

Why Did Jesus Wait?

The people at Lazarus' tomb wondered, "Couldn't Jesus have kept Lazarus from dying?"

But now, because Jesus had waited to answer Mary and Martha's prayer, he did a greater miracle than healing a sick friend. He shouted into the grave, "Lazarus, come out!" And everyone watched Lazarus come out alive after being in the grave four days!

So don't be impatient with God when you pray. Instead of demanding an answer right now, wait for God's best answer, and best time.

Picture Prayers

- Cut regular sheets of white paper into 4 squares.
- Get some markers and draw 3 pictures on the squares. (One square you will not use.)
- Draw a picture of one thing you are praying about for yourself.
- Draw a picture of one thing you are praying about for someone else.
- Draw one "thank you"-to-God picture.
- Make a poster collage of all the squares to remind you what you are praying about.

Treasure Nuggets from God's Word

"Wait for the Lord to act . . . He will honor you."

Psalm 37:34

"We wait in hope for the Lord. He helps us."

Psalm 33:20

"I was patient while I waited for the Lord. He turned to me and heard my cry for help."

Psalm 40:1

Prayer Starter

Thank you, God, for hearing every prayer. I wait for your good anwers and I trust your help with these problems _____.

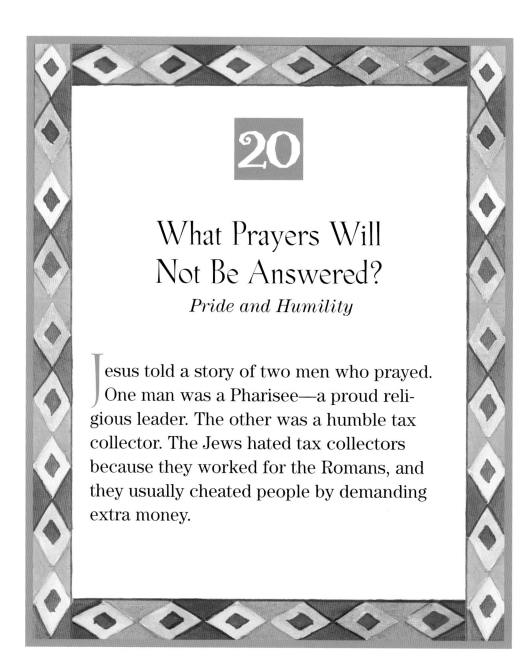

20

What Prayers Will Not Be Answered?

Pride and Humility

J esus told a story of two men who prayed. One man was a Pharisee—a proud religious leader. The other was a humble tax collector. The Jews hated tax collectors because they worked for the Romans, and they usually cheated people by demanding extra money.

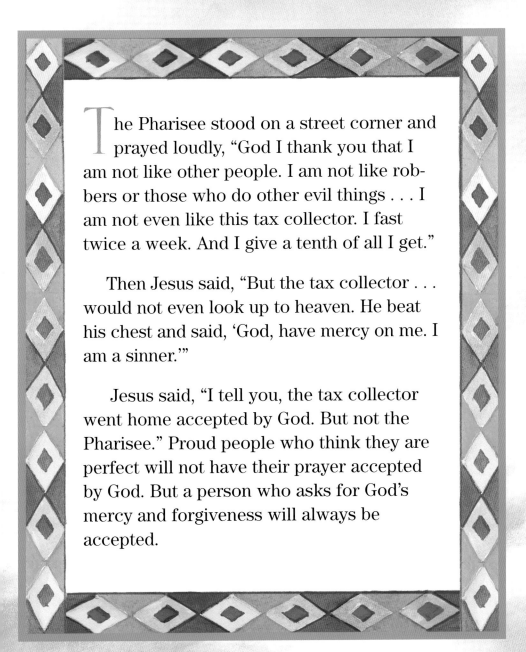

The Pharisee stood on a street corner and prayed loudly, "God I thank you that I am not like other people. I am not like robbers or those who do other evil things . . . I am not even like this tax collector. I fast twice a week. And I give a tenth of all I get."

Then Jesus said, "But the tax collector . . . would not even look up to heaven. He beat his chest and said, 'God, have mercy on me. I am a sinner.'"

Jesus said, "I tell you, the tax collector went home accepted by God. But not the Pharisee." Proud people who think they are perfect will not have their prayer accepted by God. But a person who asks for God's mercy and forgiveness will always be accepted.

Disobedience and Selfishness

If you pray while you deliberately disobey God's laws, God will not answer your prayer. The Bible says, "The Lord is far away from those who do wrong. But he hears the prayers of those who do right" (Proverbs 15:29).

God won't answer greedy or selfish requests. The Bible says, "You don't have what you want, because you don't ask God. When you do ask for something, you don't receive it . . . Because you ask for the wrong reason. You want to spend your money on your sinful pleasures" (James 4:3).

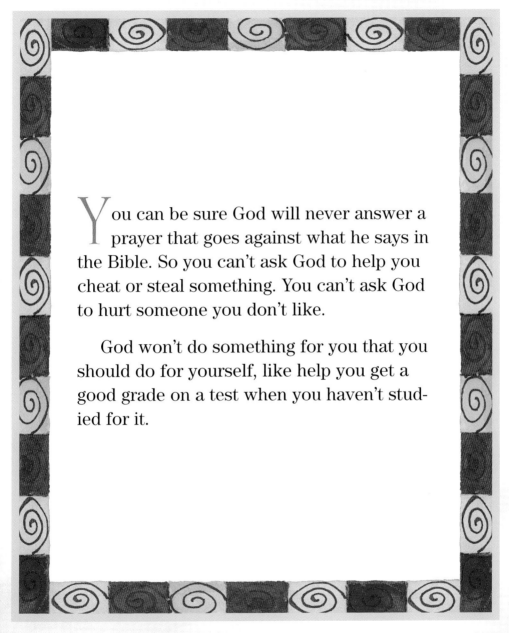

You can be sure God will never answer a prayer that goes against what he says in the Bible. So you can't ask God to help you cheat or steal something. You can't ask God to hurt someone you don't like.

God won't do something for you that you should do for yourself, like help you get a good grade on a test when you haven't studied for it.

Prayer Mobile

   Here's how to make a prayer mobile out of a plastic clothes hanger:

- Cut different shapes out of colored construction paper.
- Glue photos of people you want to pray for onto the paper shapes you have cut out. (Or draw pictures of them if you don't have a photo.)
- Punch a hole at the top of each paper shape.
- Tie various lengths of yarn through holes. Tie other end of yarn onto hanger. (Tape yarn strand on hanger to prevent sliding.)

Treasure Nuggets from God's Word

God says, "You might offer many prayers. But I will not listen to them . . . Stop doing what is wrong!"

Isaiah 1:15-16

"Who can stand in God's holy place? Anyone who has clean hands and a pure heart."

Psalms 24:3-4

"The Lord is far away from those who do wrong. But he hears the prayers of those who do right."

Proverbs 15:29

Prayer Starter

Dear God, help me do what is right. Especially help me with _____.

21

Does God Ever Say "NO" to A Prayer?

Stop and think. Have your parents ever said "No" when you've asked for something? Why did they say No? Have you ever said "No" when someone wanted you to do something?

Think of a good reason why God would say "No" to a prayer. Will a loving father or mother give a child everything she asks for? Why not?

To Whom Did God Say "NO"?

On the night before Jesus was crucified, he prayed in the Garden of Gethsemane. "Father," he said, "if you are willing, take this cup of suffering away from me. But do what you want, not what I want" (Luke 22:42).

Jesus asked God to find another way to forgive us so he didn't have to die on the cross. But Jesus was willing to obey God and go to the cross if there was no other way to save us.

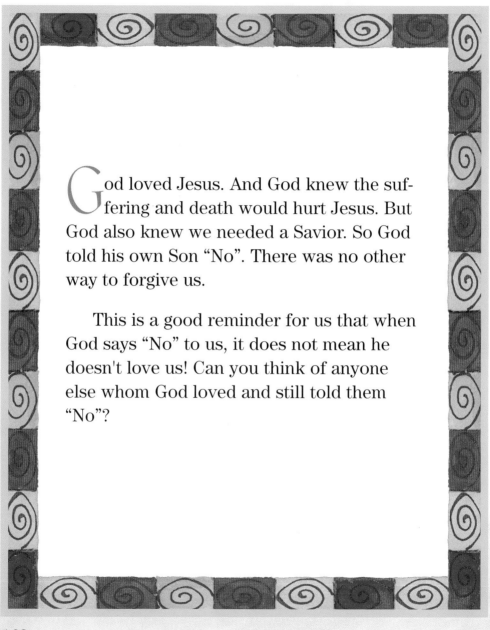

God loved Jesus. And God knew the suffering and death would hurt Jesus. But God also knew we needed a Savior. So God told his own Son "No". There was no other way to forgive us.

This is a good reminder for us that when God says "No" to us, it does not mean he doesn't love us! Can you think of anyone else whom God loved and still told them "No"?

Joseph's Troubles

When Joseph's brothers threw him down a pit and then sold him to slave traders, God did not rescue Joseph. God did not save Joseph from being a slave in Egypt or from being thrown in prison.

Joseph probably prayed for God to save him from his troubles. But God allowed the problems to happen. Why? Because God had a bigger plan that Joseph couldn't see.

God took all the wrongs done to Joseph and worked them for great good—not only for Joseph, but to save Joseph's family and many Egyptian people from starvation during seven years of famine.

Years later, Joseph understood why God hadn't rescued him from slavery or prison. He told his brothers, "You meant evil against me; but God meant it for GOOD, in order to . . . save many people" (Genesis 50:20).

Request Denied

What if God says no to your prayers? Will you still trust his love? God will always do what is best for you. If God allows something unpleasant to happen to you, remember that he has a plan—he knows how it will all turn out.

God promises to turn even things that are terrible and evil—like his Son's death on the cross—for GOOD. So we can praise God in the middle of every situation.

Do Problems Ever
End Up Being Good?

Oysters are soft little creatures that live in hard shells. As ocean water flows in and out of the oyster's shell, sometimes a grain of sand gets caught inside the shell. The sand irritates the oyster.

The oyster covers the sand with a special fluid. After a while, the sand and the fluid harden into a beautiful round object—a valuable pearl!

Lots of everyday problems bother us too, like sand bothers the little oyster. Kids say mean words. Things go wrong and accidents happen.

But God promises to work everything for good for those who love him. That's his job. Don't feel that God has let you down if God says "No" to your prayer. Trust God. Ask him to turn every problem into a blessing!

Turn It into Something Good

- Read Romans 8:38 on the next page.
- Take a lump of Play Dough in your hand.
- Now, turn the "mess" of dough into something good.
- Read the Bible verses on the next page and pray over any situation in your life that you want God to work for good.

Treasure Nuggets from God's Word

"We know that in all things God works for the good of those who love him."

Romans 8:38

"Lord, you always do what is right. My tongue will speak about it and praise you all day long."

Psalm 35:28

"Always be joyful . . . Give thanks no matter what happens."

1 Thessalonians 5:16, 18

Prayer Starter

Dear God, help me to trust you, even when things go wrong. Please take all these problems and turn them into something good _____.

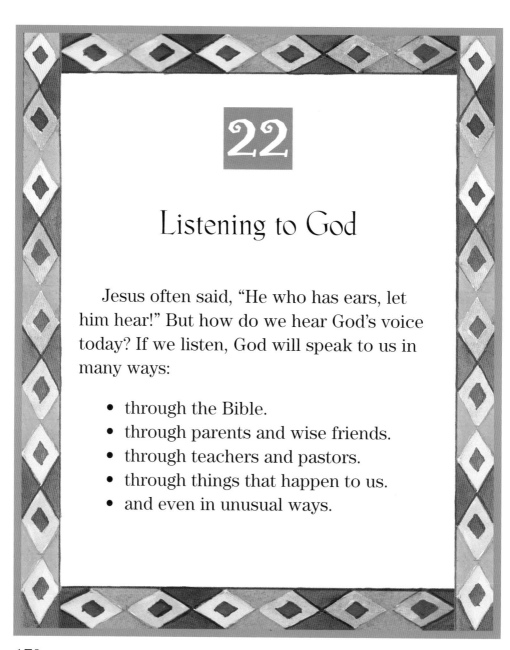

22

Listening to God

Jesus often said, "He who has ears, let him hear!" But how do we hear God's voice today? If we listen, God will speak to us in many ways:

- through the Bible.
- through parents and wise friends.
- through teachers and pastors.
- through things that happen to us.
- and even in unusual ways.

In the Bible God used angels, miracles, dreams, and visions to speak to people. God can still do that today. God can speak anytime and anywhere and in any way he wants.

Most of the time God speaks to us when we read or listen to the Bible. God's Word tells us about God's love and promises. The Bible helps us know how God wants us to live.

A Boy Who Talked and Listened to God

When George Washington Carver was a boy, he learned that God hears and answers prayer. Once George prayed for a carving knife so he could make things out of wood. Then he dreamed of a knife stuck in a watermelon.

The next day George walked to a watermelon field. Guess what he found—a watermelon with a knife in it!

When George grew up, he asked God to show him the wonders of the whole universe. God told George, "No. But I'll show you the wonders of the peanut."

So George talked with God and listened to God. When George experimented with peanuts, God helped him. And guess what! George discovered three hundred different products that could be made from peanuts!

Who Heard God Speak?

1 Samuel 3:1-19

One night when Samuel was a boy, he heard God call his name. Samuel thought Eli the priest was calling him. So he went to Eli.

But Eli said he had not called Samuel. After this happened three times, Eli told Samuel, "Go and lie down. If someone calls out to you again, say, 'Speak Lord. I'm listening.'" So Samuel went back to his bed. Soon he heard, "Samuel! Samuel!" He answered, "Speak. I'm listening."

Then God told Samuel what would happen in the future. As Samuel grew up, God was with him. God made everything Samuel said come true.

Elijah Hears A Whisper

Kings 19:1-19

When the evil Queen Jezebel threatened to kill Elijah, he was afraid. He ran for his life and went into a cave. God came to him and said, "Go out and stand on the mountain. I am going to pass by."

As God came by, a powerful wind tore the mountains apart and broke up the rocks. After the wind there was an earthquake. God wasn't in the earthquake. After the earthquake came a fire. God wasn't in any of these things.

Then God spoke to Elijah in a gentle whisper. When Elijah heard the whisper, he went to the entrance of the cave. God told him to go back home because there was work for him to do. So Elijah did what God said.

Sit and Listen

Do you ever talk to God in prayer and then forget to listen? The Lord says, "Be still and know that I am God" (Psalm 46:10).

- Take time to read the Bible verses on the next page.
- Sit quietly—relax in God's presence.
- Listen for God to give you a new thought.
- Listen for God's idea of how to do something.
- Silently pray what God puts on your mind.

Treasure Nuggets from God's Word

"Those who have ears should listen."
Revelation 2:29

"Listen to God's voice today. If you hear it, don't be stubborn."
Psalm 95:7

Jesus said, "My sheep listen to my voice. I know them, and they follow me."
John 10:27

Prayer Starter

Dear God, I'm glad you never stop loving me. I just want to sit here quietly with you. Help me listen for your voice.

USE YOUR BIBLE TO PRAY:

The Bible is full of prayers, especially in the Psalms. When you pray, you can use your Bible.

- Look up the verses.

- Read and think about each verse.

- Ask: What does this verse mean to me?

- Let the words become your prayers as you talk to God.

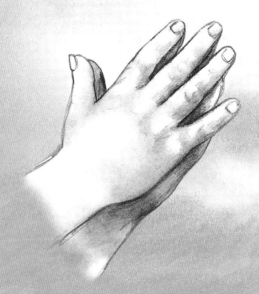

To help you pray, ... *pray Matthew 7:7-11*

To help you praise God, ... *pray Psalm 100:1-2,*
Psalm 150:1-6

To remember God's love, ... *pray John 3:16,*
Psalm 145:8-21

To remember Jesus' gift, ... *pray Isaiah 53:1-12*

To look forward to heaven, *pray Revelation 21 and 22*

To be encouraged, ... *pray Ephesians 3:14-21*

To not give up, ... *pray Galatians 6:9-10*

To live for God, ...*pray Romans 12:1-16*

In times of stress, ...*pray Philippians 4:6-9*

When you feel thankful, ...*pray Psalm 118:1*

When you feel worried, ...*pray Philippians 4:6-7,*
1 Peter 5:7

When you face troubles, . . .*pray Psalm 46:1-3, 10-11*

When you feel sorrowful, ...*pray Psalm 42:5, 8, 11*

When you feel fearful, ...*pray Psalm 23*

When you feel angry, ...*pray James 1:19-20*

When you have disobeyed, ...*pray 1 John 1:9,*
                                        Psalm 51:9-12

When you need help, ...*pray Psalm 37:4*

When you are sick, ...*pray James 5:13-15*

When you feel tired, ...*pray Isaiah 40:28-31*

When a loved one dies, .*pray 1 Thessalonians 4:13-18*

When you want to get even, . . .*pray Romans 12:19-21*

The CHAIN of PRAYER

This Prayer Chain helps children structure their prayers to God. It offers pre-schoolers a visual "help" for praying.

- Cut paper strips (2 x 4 inches) from red, yellow, and blue construction paper.

- Cut two strips (2 x 4 inches) from white paper.

- Use markers to color a rainbow on one of the white paper strips.

- Explain the meaning of the colors as you link the stripes and tape them into a chain.

For children who read, write these words on the appropriate links:

"Dear God (on white), I Thank You (on blue), I Pray for Many Needs (on rainbow), I Love You, God (on red), and I Pray in Jesus' Name (on yellow).

WHITE – is for God. We come to God in prayer and call him by name: Dear God, Dear Father, Dear Lord, etc. White reminds us that God is holy.

BLUE – is for thankfulness. Thank God for families, friends, health, and for his love and forgiveness. Blue reminds us of the blue sky God made.

RAINBOW – (multicolored strip) is for the rainbow. This reminds us to pray for ourselves and for many people in the world with many needs. A rainbow reminds us of God's care.

RED – is for love. We tell God how much we love him. We thank him for his love and for sending Jesus. Red reminds us of the love of God.

YELLOW – is the color of sunshine. It also reminds us of Jesus, the SON of God. When we end our prayers, we say, "In Jesus' name, I pray. Amen." Yellow reminds us of Jesus, God's Son.

Hang the Prayer Chain by your child's bed where it is easily seen. Refer to it during your next prayer times. Your child will learn the meaning of each color and a pattern of prayer.

The LORD'S PRAYER

When Jesus taught his disciples
to pray, he used this prayer as an
example of how to pray

(Matthew 6:9-13).

Our Father in heaven,

may your name be honored.

May your kingdom come.

May what you want to happen be done

on earth as it is done in heaven.

Give us today our daily bread.

Forgive us our sins

as we also have forgiven
those who sin against us.

Keep us from falling into sin
when we are tempted.

Save us from the evil one.

The
End

We want to hear from you. Please send your comments about this
book to us in care of the address below. Thank you.

Zonder**kidz**™

Grand Rapids, MI 49530
www.zonderkidz.com